SHAKE RAG

FROM THE LIFE OF ELVIS PRESLEY

WRITTEN BY Amy Littlesugar

ILLUSTRATED BY Floyd Cooper

PHILOMEL BOOKS

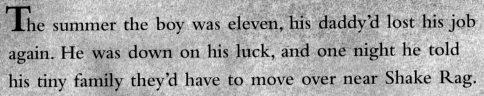

The summer the boy was eleven, his daddy'd lost his job again. He was down on his luck, and one night he told his tiny family they'd have to move over near Shake Rag.

Mostly black people lived there. A few whites too. But what they all shared was that they were poor.

The boy's mama cried when she saw the place. She didn't want him growing up so close to the tracks or near those dark and smoky jukehouse joints, where the music swirled out on the streets and there was dancing 'till dawn.

More than that though, she didn't want the boy hearing what some folks in the other part of town had to say about them: that they were "white trash."

But the boy already knew that. He'd heard it at school, especially when he wore those hand-me-down overalls or his belly rumbled out loud in class (no one knew all he'd had for supper the night before was cornbread and water).

And some days, when the boy'd help his friend John Allen Cooke tote groceries from the back of his pick-up truck, he was sure he could hear some kids call, "Look! There's that white trash."

They stayed away from that boy. Even when his daddy got a better job, trucking canned goods for Mr. McCarty, the grocer. Even when they moved to a bigger house near Shake Rag. Those kids from the other side of town turned up their noses at him.

So he started carrying this little old guitar mostly everywhere he went. Maybe to keep him company.

Now the boy loved that guitar. His mama'd scraped to get it for him secondhand at the hardware store, and Brother Smith, the pastor from where they used to live, he'd come over and show the boy how to play a few chords on it. That guitar might be old and beat-up, but when you strummed those strings, it sounded like it could wake up the world!

And when the boy cradled it close, when he began to sing, his sadness went wandering. His loneliness too. And he got to dreaming he was a sparkling cowboy star like Red Foley or Bill Monroe—on stage at the Grand Ole Opry in Nashville, Tennessee.

Or he'd dream about Beale Street, way off in the big city
of Memphis. The boy's daddy hoped to find work there one
day. Good work. And the boy hoped so too, because Beale
Street was where the great bluesmen lived!

The boy'd close his eyes and in no time he'd be jamming
with Mr. Arthur "Big Boy" Crudup himself:

> *"Well, that's all right,—Mama,—that's all right for you.*
> *That's all right,—Mama, just—an-yway you do!"*

"Boy," Mr. Crudup might say when their guitars stopped
ringing, "I think you gonna be famous one day!"

The boy's mama worried though. Dreaming about Nashville was fine. Didn't he just sound like an angel when he sat by the radio singing "Blue Moon of Kentucky"?

But singing the blues was something else. It was field hollers and street shouts. His mama had to say it—it was not their kind of music.

And even though their neighbors near Shake Rag had been real good to them, giving them handouts like food and clothes when times were tough, how'd it look? A white boy, her boy, singing that way!

The boy's mama decided. There'd be none of that music in her house. Not Blind Willie Johnson. Not the Soul Stirrers. Not Charley Patton neither.

And if the good Lord saw fit, the boy's daddy'd get their old green Plymouth running soon. Get them away from Shake Rag. Get them to some big city like Memphis where Daddy could find work.

Then one day a traveling church came to town. It called itself the Sanctified Church, but it was really nothing more than a broken down, patched up old tent. Underneath were a few rickety benches and an upright piano that had seen better days.

That preacher stood outside in the sunshine, inviting everyone to come on in and sing to God.

"It's 'good news' music we got in here," he called as people walked by, "gospel music. Lifts y'up when y'feelin' down!"

Some people though, black as well as white, felt the Sanctified Church was not respectable. They didn't think much of that bluesy piano playing or the soft wail of a horn on the hot night air.

And they didn't take kindly to the scatter and crash of the tambourine or guitars in church for that matter either. It was all the devil's music!

But the boy's eyes widened with wonder when he heard it. He knew his mama'd never let him go there. But maybe he'd just sneak over there when his mama wasn't looking.

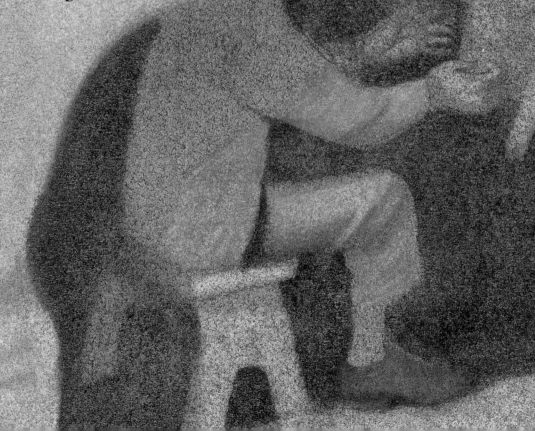

Now those who came regular to the Sanctified Church really dressed up for the Lord. They wore their finest feathers and their fanciest shoes, and they were there to be happy, not sad. Loved, not lonely. They were there to sing and forget their troubles, and Preacher always got them going.

He'd start out soft:

"*Precious Lord, take my hand,*
Lead me on, let me stand."

Then he'd loosen his collar and let his voice grow—

"*I am tired, I am weak, I am WORN...!!*"

That first night the boy made it to the Sanctified Church
he stood alone at the back of the tent, and his heart raced.

Someone was playing a blues number on the old upright;
fingers traveling up and down the keys, elbows helping out.
He heard that tambourine scatter, "Hushakke!!!", and the soft
wail of a horn on the hot night air.

And all around him, the people rocked and swayed, their
hands soaring toward heaven.

But it was the guitar player whom the boy really watched.

A big man, his face shiny with sweat, he hugged that guitar and strummed away all his sadness and his loneliness, making those strings sob and cry. And when he was through, the sound of his song still hung on the air.

"Praise God," someone wept. "Amen!"

And the boy stared in wonder as he never had before.

As often as the Sanctified Church came that summer, the boy stole away to visit. He learned "good news" music was field hollers and street shouts—the same kind of music that swirled out on the streets and lasted 'till dawn in Shake Rag.

And he didn't stand way in the back of that old tent by himself anymore either.

His hands stung from clapping; his feet from stomping. But just like Preacher said, he was lifted up...

And he didn't mind so much when school started that fall and the traveling church moved on for winter.

The boy had that "good news" music with him, and most times, slung over his shoulder, his best friend too. Only there were still those kids who whispered and laughed at him, and he felt their words.

"Look! There's that white trash."

Then one afternoon when no one was around, some of the biggest, the roughest town boys jumped him. They had seen him many times, off to himself, playing that little old guitar. They knew what it meant to him, but they'd fix that. And no one saw them cut the first string, or the second, or the third, and throw that guitar to the ground.

The boy was left alone with his broken guitar.

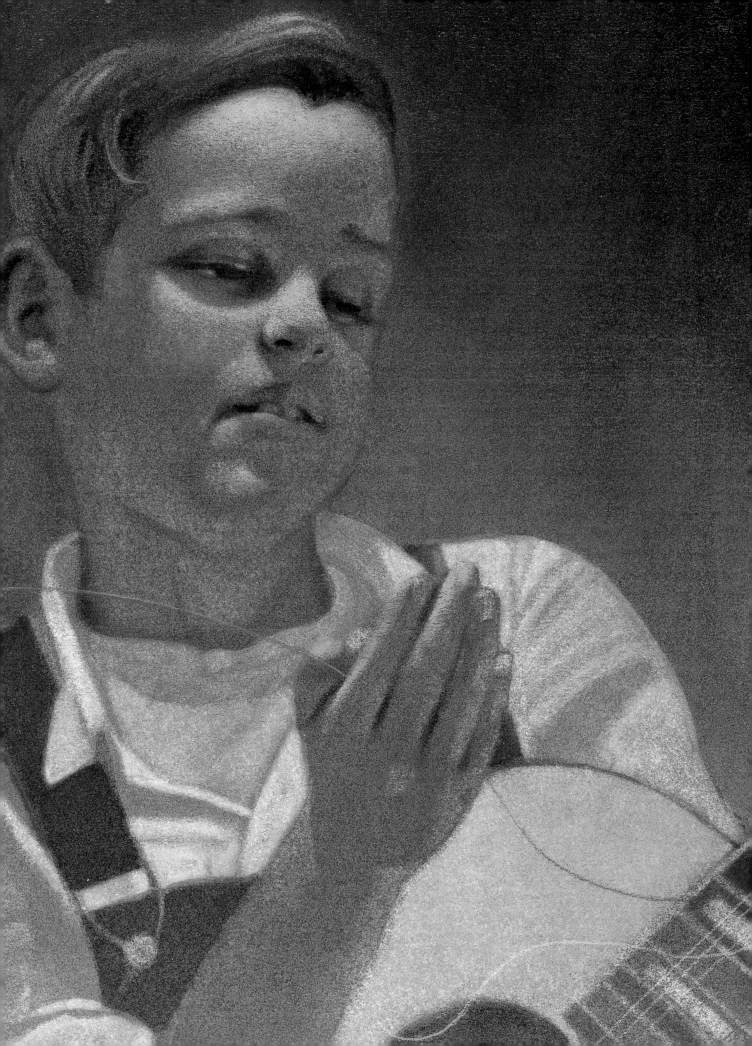

He wished he could show them—all of them, the kids at school, even Mama and Daddy—the way music made him feel.

But how?

The boy's mind drifted. He imagined summer'd come again, and the Sanctified Church was back, and the big man with the guitar too. Only this time the boy stood right beside him, and his guitar wasn't old and beat up, but shiny and new. And when the boy strummed across that guitar, the big man grinned. And everyone looked up—took notice.

The boy sat quiet and still. That was it! he thought. That was his real dream. He'd play for them. Really play for them. No matter how many broken guitars it took—Amen!

Days passed, and some other town kids stopped by. They'd heard the awful thing that'd happened to the boy's guitar. And surprise of surprises! They'd chipped in to buy it new strings.

The boy thanked them in his shy way. He didn't tell them his daddy'd finally got the Plymouth running. It would make it to the big city. To Memphis, Tennessee, God-willing.

So on a cold November morning near Shake Rag, the boy's mama began packing boxes and such. People came to buy their table and chairs. Already Shake Rag seemed very far away.

But the boy knew he had something left to do. The next day he slung his guitar over his shoulder and carried it to school once more.

At recess, a bunch of kids—some of the very ones that had broken the strings—crowded 'round him when he told them he wanted to give a small concert before he left.

He played a couple of songs. And then, for the last one, he took and held his guitar so close, his hair fell in his eyes, and he began to sing a song about the leaves on a tree and the green grass growing all around.

His voice, sweet and high, quavered at first. But then, it grew strong, reaching out to those who listened—every one of them.

This time, no one whispered, and no one laughed.

And when the boy was through, the sound of his song still hung on the air.

"Elvis," he heard a kid say, kind of like Mr. Arthur "Big Boy" Crudup had in his dreams, "I think you're gonna be famous one day!"

That night, the boy walked on over to Shake Rag. In
the darkness, under the glow of a streetlamp, he could hear
a bluesy piano playing and the soft wail of a horn on the
night air. He could hear women laughing and men singing,
and for a moment, he wished it was summer again, and he
was standing in the back of the Sanctified Church.

But then he remembered: The Plymouth was waiting.
The big city, too.

And he was ready. Ready to wake up the world.

ONE SUMMER DAY...

In 1954, nineteen-year-old Elvis Presley was asked to come sing for Sun Records, a small company with a studio near downtown Memphis. Sporting sideburns, holes in his socks, and that old secondhand guitar, he was still very poor and very shy. But music meant everything to him, and this was his big chance. So he sang and he sang, one song after another.

Sam Phillips, owner of Sun Records, sat in his control room frowning. "Take a break," he said at last.

Elvis was disappointed. Frustrated too.

Then suddenly, out of nowhere, a feeling got hold of him.

Before anyone realized what was happening, he was singing again. Only, this song was different.

It made backup guitarists Scotty Moore and Bill Black want to fall in behind him. Elvis was singing "That's All Right, Mama," an old blues number by Arthur "Big Boy" Crudup.

Sam Phillips was surprised. Surprised that Elvis, a white kid, even knew it. He had no idea of the lonely boy who once hung around Shake Rag; who dreamed and listened late at night to Memphis's first black radio station, WDIA; who made everyone in his house hush when Mahalia Jackson, the queen of gospel, came singing over the airwaves just to him.

Sam Phillips scrambled to get Elvis's scared, yearning voice on tape. It was raw but it was fresh. And it was filled with passion. Both black and white. For as long as he lived, Elvis Presley never forgot what the people of Shake Rag had shared with him—their music.

Sam nodded. It was the sound of a brand-new day.

BIBLIOGRAPHY

Bane, Michael. *White Boy Singin' the Blues.* New York: Da Capo Press, 1992.

Barlow, William. *Looking Up at Down: The Emergence of Blues Culture.* Philadelphia: Temple University Press, 1989.

Broughton, Viv. B*lack Gospel: An Illustrated History of the Gospel Sound.* Dorset, England: Blandford Press, 1985.

Clayton, Rose, and Dick Heard. *Elvis Up Close: In the Words of Those Who Knew Him Best.* Atlanta: Turner Publishing, Inc., 1994.

Dundy, Elaine. *Elvis and Gladys.* New York: Macmillan Publishing Company, 1985.

Gaillard, Frye. *Watermelon Wine.* New York: St. Martin's Press, 1978.

Guralnick, Peter. *Last Train to Memphis.* Boston: Little, Brown & Company, 1994.

Higginsen, Vy. *This Is My Song: A Collection of Gospel Music for the Family.* New York: Crown Publishers, Inc., 1995.

Hill, Thomas A. *The Guitar.* New York: Franklin Watts, 1973.

Hudson, Wade, and Cheryl L. *How Sweet the Sound: African-American Songs for Children.* New York: Scholastic, Inc., 1995.

Levine, Lawrence. *Black Culture and Black Consciousness: Afro-American Folk Thought from Slavery to Freedom.* New York: Oxford University Press, 1978.

Marcus, Greil. *Mystery Train: Images of America in Rock 'n' Roll.* New York: Penguin Books USA, Inc., 1990.

Pierce, Patricia Jobe. *The Ultimate Elvis.* New York: Simon & Schuster, 1994.

Public Broadcasting Service. *That Rhythm, Those Blues: The American Experience* (videotape).

Robinson, Louie. "The Truth About the Elvis Presley Rumor." Jet Magazine, August 1, 1957, pp. 58-61.

Southern, Eileen. *The Music of Black Americans: A History.* New York: W. W. Norton & Company, 1971.

The pre-teen-aged Elvis Presley would have been introduced through radio broadcasts of the time, to many musical influences. These included, because of his southern connections, the Grand Ole Opry in Nashville, gospel music, and the popular Beale Street Memphis blues sound.

Patricia Lee Gauch, Editor

Text copyright © 1998 by Amy Littlesugar. Illustrations copyright © 1998 by Floyd Cooper. All rights reserved. This book, or parts thereof, may not be reproduced in any form without permission in writing from the publisher, Philomel Books, a division of The Putnam & Grosset Group, 200 Madison Avenue, New York, NY 10016. Philomel Books, Reg. U.S. Pat. & Tm. Off. Published simultaneously in Canada. Printed in Hong Kong by South China Printing Co. (1988) Ltd. Book design by Donna Mark. Text set in Bembo Semibold. Library of Congress Cataloging-in-Publication Data. Littlesugar, Amy. Shake Rag / Amy Littlesugar; illustrated by Floyd Cooper. p. cm. Includes bibliographical references. Summary: A story about a period in the childhood of Elvis Presley when his family was dirt poor and he was introduced to the soulful music of the Sanctified Church that travelled to his town. [1. Presley, Elvis, 1935-1977—Fiction. 2. Singers—Fiction. 3. Afro-Americans—Music—Fiction.] I. Cooper, Floyd, ill. II. Title.PZ7.L7362Sh 1998 [E]—dc21 97-9618 CIP AC ISBN 0-399-23005-X   10 9 8 7 6 5 4 3 2 1   FIRST IMPRESSION